WITH THANKS TO
RACHEL BODEN

AND THE USUAL HUGS
FOR MONIKA AND LUKA

www.davidmelling.co.uk

www.huglessdouglas.co.uk

HODDER CHILDREN'S BOOKS

First published in Great Britain in 2015
by Hodder and Stoughton

This paperback edition published in 2017

Text and illustrations copyright © David Melling, 2015

The moral rights of the author have been asserted.

All rights reserved

A CIP catalogue record for this book
is available from the British Library.

ISBN: 978 1 444 94904 9

10 9 8 7 6 5 4 3 2

Printed and bound in China

MIX
Paper from
responsible sources
FSC
www.fsc.org   FSC® C104740

Hodder Children's Books
An imprint of Hachette Children's Group
Part of Hodder and Stoughton
Carmelite House
50 Victoria Embankment
London EC4Y 0DZ
An Hachette UK Company

www.hachette.co.uk
www.hachettechildrens.co.uk

HUGLESS DOUGLAS

goes to LITTLE SCHOOL

David Melling

Hodder
Children's
Books

The sun was shining on another BIG DAY for Douglas!

He had just joined the Walking Bus on his first day at Little School. 'I wonder what we're going to do?' said Douglas. 'I can't wait!'

'Good morning, everyone!' trilled their new teacher.
'My name is Miss Moo-Hoo!

Can you hang your bags on the pegs please, and sit down nicely?'

Not everyone could reach, so Douglas lent a hand.

'Ooh, thank you, Douglas,'
said Miss Moo-Hoo,
'you **are** helpful!'

Douglas felt a **TICKLE** inside his **TUMMY**
and it made him feel very happy.

'Now tell me,' said Miss Moo-Hoo, 'what do you all like doing best?'

Every answer was different:

Douglas still felt the nice tickle in his tummy and thought it would be helpful to **show** Miss Moo-Hoo exactly what he liked doing best…

'Oh my!' gasped Miss Moo-Hoo.
'What a BIG HUG!'

'Douglas has a lovely idea,' she said.
'Let's all give each other a gentle
HELLO HUG!'

So they did.

Douglas was having so much hugging fun! He called them

HELPFUL HUGS

and everyone got one.

He even showed the class what to do in a
HUG EMERGENCY,
with as many cushions
as he could...

which was a
surprise to some!

Eventually, Miss Moo-Hoo
settled them down by the tree.
'Let's make a colourful picture,' she said.

'Look at us making bottom prints!' said Douglas.

They all splished and splashed their way to lunchtime.

'Don't forget to wash before you eat!'
called Miss Moo-Hoo.

'You've got red feet!' said Douglas.
'Your tummy is green!' said Splosh.

So they grabbed their water bottles and SQUIRTED...

and everything got a bit **SoGGY.**

When, at last, they were clean and dry,

Douglas and Splosh ate their lunch together, now the best of friends.

After lunch, Miss Moo-Hoo
got out the climbing blocks.
'Come on, Douglas, let's
build a tower!' said Splosh.

Everyone soon joined in and
the tower grew and grew.
And the more it grew, the more it
WIBBLED and WOBBLED
in all the wrong places

until...

down came the lot!

'WHEEEEEEEEEEE!'

Douglas leapt into the air...

and caught everyone!

'Well done, Douglas!' said Miss Moo-Hoo.

'That was brilliant!'
said Splosh,
flapping his wings.

'It's home time now,'
Miss Moo-Hoo said.
'Collect your things,
please, and get ready
for the Walking Bus.'

As they set off Douglas felt his happy tummy feeling. And when Splosh asked him why he was smiling, it turned out his new friend had the same feeling too!

'LITTLE SCHOOL
IS SO MUCH FUN!'
they laughed.

Sandpit

Wash and Tidy-up

Not Snack Time

Naughty Step

First Day Hug

First Aid Corner

Nap Time

Story Time

Will-You-Be-My-Friend
Hug

Dressing Up

Painting Skittles

CRAZY COUNTING

Douglas loves counting at Little School and there are lots of fun things to count in this story. See if you can find...

1 SHEEP ON A SCOOTER

2 MOOSE ANTLERS

3 FRIENDS IN A SANDPIT

4 FRIENDS WASHING UP

5 FRIENDS HAVING A NAP

6 SHEEP IN A TOWER

7 BUTTERFLIES

8 DAISIES

9 PAINT POTS

10 HUGS